D1584741

Virus

by

Tommy Donbavand

Illustrated by Dan Chernett

Essex County Council

3013020268734 8

To Claire and Stuart

Our books are tested
for children and young people by
children and young people.

Thanks to everyone who consulted on
a manuscript for their time and effort in
helping us to make our books better
for our readers.

First published in 2012 in Great Britain by
Barrington Stoke Ltd
18 Walker St, Edinburgh, EH3 7LP

www.barringtonstoke.co.uk

Copyright © 2012 Tommy Donbavand
Illustrations © Dan Chernett

The moral right of the author has been asserted in
accordance with the Copyright, Designs and
Patents Act 1988

ISBN: 978-1-78112-000-2

Printed in China by Leo

Contents

Chapter 1
A Site for Sore Eyes

M – y –

...

W – e – b – s – i – t – e –

...

b – y –

M –

...

...

"Where's the letter 'a'?" asked Max.

Nahim snatched the computer keyboard away from him before he could type any more. Why on Earth had Mr Lee made Nahim be Max's partner? Max was such a loser!

"Hey!" said Max. "Mr Lee said we had to work together on this project!"

"If you want to waste the next hour copying and pasting pictures, why don't you go and work with the girls over there?" Nahim asked. He turned to Amina and Polly who were working at the next desk. They were busy typing text and adding links to their own website.

"Do you two want to do a swap?" Nahim called out.

"What kind of swap?" asked Polly.

Nahim grinned. "You get Max, and I get a bit of peace to do something better than this stupid 'build your first website' rubbish!"

"Nahim!" Mr Lee bellowed from the other side of the room. "I have had enough of your lip! See me after class!"

Amina and Polly grinned as Nahim slumped back in his chair with a face like thunder.

"I can't work with the girls anyway," said Max. "They go to stage school on Saturday mornings. I don't want to make a website about dancing."

Nahim rolled his eyes. "So what do you want to make a website about?"

"War Zone World," said Max, with a huge smile. "You know, the role-playing game where you make your own avatar and go on adventures? My mum lets me play it on-line every night for an hour after I've done my homework. I'm a 9th level wizard!"

"You're a 9th level loser!" muttered Nahim. He checked that Mr Lee wasn't watching, then opened a new Internet window and began to type.

"What are you doing?" said Max. "Mr Lee said we weren't to look at any other websites. He said you could get a virus, and – "

"You only get viruses if you click on links you don't know, stupid," Nahim hissed. "But you've given me an idea ..."

Nahim grabbed his schoolbag and began to root through the broken pens and sweet papers at the bottom. "Please be there," he said to himself. "Please be there ... Yes!"

Nahim pulled out what he was looking for – a USB flash drive. He smiled, pushed the drive into a spare slot and went back to typing. A few seconds later he attached a file called **thunderstrike.exe** to an e-mail.

Max stared at the screen. "What's that?" he asked.

"A little treat to show Polly and Amina what they get for laughing at me," said Nahim. Once the file was attached, he changed the name to **showtune.mp3**.

Max gasped, his eyes wide. "That's a virus, isn't it?" he said. "You've sent the girls a computer virus that looks like a song they can use on their website!"

Nahim spun to face him. "Keep your voice down!" he hissed. "I don't want Loony Lee over here before I'm done!"

"But the school computers are all linked together," said Max. "If the girls open that virus, every PC in this room will get infected."

"Not just in this room," said Nahim. "If I've written this thing right, the whole school network will grind to a halt – and they'll trace it all back to the computer the girls were using!"

He clicked 'send'.

Amina was typing the details of the next stage school show onto her website – it was going to be *The Wizard of Oz*. Just then, a window popped up on her screen. "**Showtune.mp3**?" she read. "Is this yours, Polly?"

Her friend peered at the screen. "Well, I did download some music," she said, and reached for the mouse.

Amina pulled at Polly's hand before Polly could click on the link. "Wait!" she said. "Your music file is still in the download window." She spun in her chair to face Nahim. "You sent this to us," she said, "didn't you?"

Nahim tried to look innocent. "Sent what to you?"

"You're such a liar!" Amina said. "I bet this is a virus, and you sent it to us so we'd open it and infect every computer in this room!"

"Not just this room – " Max began.

"Shut up, geek!" Nahim snapped.

"Well, I know what to do with this," said Amina, and turned back to her computer. "I'll forward it to Mr Lee so he can take a look at it."

Nahim dived for the girls' computer. "You're not going to do that!" he hissed. He grabbed the mouse and reached his finger out over the left button.

"He's trying to open the virus!" Amina said to Polly and Max. She clamped her hand down on top of Nahim's. "If he does that, we'll be the ones in trouble!"

Max looked over his shoulder, sure that Mr Lee would hear the racket and come running any second.

Click. Beep ... Beep ... Beep ...

Max turned back towards the sound, and his jaw dropped open.

Nahim, Polly and Amina had vanished.

Chapter 2
Trapped in the Web

Nahim, Amina and Polly looked round in horror.

They were in a room where everything – even the floor – was painted yellow. There were black patterns all over the bricks on the back wall.

"What happened?" Amina gulped.

"I don't know," said Polly. "The classroom just vanished …"

Amina spun to face Nahim. "What did you do?" she demanded.

"Nothing!" yelled Nahim. He started to back away. "This has got nothing to do with me!"

"It must have!" Amina said. "Everything was fine till you opened that virus! Now it's made everything vanish!"

"Viruses can't do that!" said Nahim. "They can't affect the real world."

"Well, the real world is nowhere to be seen," said Amina. Her voice was low and angry. "And I'm sure it's your fault."

Polly took a few timid steps over the yellow ground. "Hello?" she called out. "Is there anybody there?"

There was no reply.

Polly slumped back against the patterned bricks and sniffed like she was trying not to cry. "Where are we?" she asked in a tiny voice.

Amina rushed over to Polly and put her arm around her. "I don't know," she admitted. "But I'm going to find out."

Then all of a sudden, Nahim gasped. "Is your stage school show *The Wizard of Oz*?" he asked.

Amina looked at him as if he'd gone crazy. "Yes," she said. "Why?"

Nahim pointed to where Amina and Polly were sitting. "Those bricks behind you – they've each got a letter printed on."

Amina ran her fingers over the bricks. There was a letter on each one – the letters

stuck out from the brick by a few centimetres. "He's right, Polly," she said. "They go all the way up to the roof."

Look," said Nahim, and pointed at the wall. "If you read it from the left end of the wall, it says: 'Our next show will be *The Wizard of Oz*. There will be try-outs on Saturday 28th'."

Polly wiped her nose on her sleeve and joined the others to look at the bricks. "I typed that onto our website before the rest of the world vanished."

Amina bent down to read the line below: "'You must be ready to dance at 10am. Please wear loose clothes'."

"I typed that as well," said Polly.

"Then I think I know where we are!" cried Nahim.

"Where?" Amina asked.

Nahim grinned. "We're inside your website!"

"We can't be inside a website!" said Polly. "How can that even happen?"

"I don't know," said Nahim. "But somehow it has! This is wicked!"

"This is some sort of joke, isn't it?" Amina snapped.

"What do you mean?" asked Nahim.

Amina glared at him. "You've found a way to hide the classroom and trick us into thinking we've been dragged inside the Internet."

Nahim rolled his eyes. "You think that somehow I got everyone to leave the room, then painted everything yellow and built a wall made out of the exact letters you had just typed onto your website – all in a few seconds? Yeah, right."

Amina's face grew pale. When Nahim put it like that, it did sound stupid. "OK," she said at last. "So – somehow – we've been dragged inside our own website. The question is – how do we get back out?"

"Who cares?" asked Nahim. "This is cool! We're the first people ever to go inside the Internet! We're like the first men to walk on the moon!"

"There's one big difference," said Amina. "The first men on the moon knew how to get back home again."

This time, Polly did start to cry. "You mean we're going to be stuck here forever?" she sobbed.

Amina gave her a hug. "No, we're not," she told her. "We'll find a way back to school, I promise. Won't we, Nahim?"

"Are you two crazy?" Nahim asked. "We can't go back yet! Just think of all the different websites we've got to explore first – video sites, on-line games, message boards ... We could go anywhere in the world!"

"The only place we want to go is back to Mr Lee's class," said Amina. "And you're going to help us."

"Me?" said Nahim. "What makes you think I know how to – ?"

And that's when the ground began to shake.

Chapter 3
Climb or Die

The whole website shook from side to side, till it was hard for the children to stay on their feet.

"What's doing this?" Polly screamed. She grabbed Amina's arm and held on.

Nahim pointed to one side. "Er ... I think it's that thing," he gulped.

The girls stared in horror. "What is that?" demanded Amina.

There was a giant monster stomping towards them. Its face was twisted, like an angry bull's, but with sharp vampire teeth. It was covered with scaly grey skin and horns grew from the top of its head. The monster stopped in front of the children and stared down at them. Its eyes blazed red.

"I **am your ruler!**" the monster roared. Steam shot out of its nose. "**You will serve me!**"

In spite of his fear, Nahim found that he could speak. "Who are you?"

The beast threw back its head and roared. "**I am the master of this domain! I am Thunderstrike!**"

"Oh no," said Nahim in a tiny voice.

"What is it?" asked Amina.

Nahim stared up at Thunderstrike in terror. "It's my computer virus!"

Amina stared up at the bull-like monster as it scraped its hooves across the yellow floor, spraying out a shower of golden sparks. "That's your virus?"

Nahim nodded. "That's what I called it when I wrote it – Thunderstrike!"

"Then you're an idiot!" Amina said.

"**Kneel down!**" bellowed Thunderstrike.

"Why should we?" asked Nahim, and took a nervous step forward.

Amina tried to pull him back. "What are you doing?" she hissed.

"Getting us out of here!" Nahim stepped up to the monster again. "I made you!" he yelled. "I made you from lines of computer code. I am **your** master, and you will do what I say!"

Thunderstrike's eyes blazed with fury. He opened his mouth to reveal a long, wet tongue, and roared. Nahim was covered from head to toe with gloopy strings of sticky, green saliva.

"Oh, yuck!" Nahim wiped the globs of warm spit from his face.

"Any other bright ideas?" Amina asked, behind him.

"Just one," said Nahim. "Climb!"

Nahim raced to the back wall and found a foot-hold on one of the letter bricks that stuck out from the wall. He began to climb.

The girls followed as fast as they could, as Thunderstrike stomped after them.

"Hurry!" cried Amina. "We have to get higher!"

Thunderstrike reached the wall and swung a massive paw up at the children. One of his claws hit Amina's shoe and tore a hole in the black leather.

The children climbed higher and higher, while Thunderstrike stared at them from the ground below.

"Why isn't he following us?" whispered Polly.

"He's too big," Nahim said. "He can't grip onto the bricks to pull himself up."

Just then, the wall rocked. The children clung on tight. Below them, they saw Thunderstrike start to rip bricks out of the wall, tearing out holes big enough for his giant hands and feet. He began to climb after them.

"Sometimes I wish you'd keep your mouth shut, Nahim!" Amina yelled.

Thunderstrike moved fast, his fists tearing out brick after brick as he climbed the wall. The children could feel his scorching breath as he got closer.

At last, Nahim reached the top row of text and sat on it. He reached down to help pull Amina and Polly up.

"What now?" Polly asked.

Nahim looked up at a line of red text above his head. "These are your links, aren't they?" he asked.

Amina nodded. "They were the first things we put on our website."

"Then we grab hold of one of them," said Nahim. "If we're lucky, it should send us to another website where we'll be safe."

"If we're lucky?" cried Amina. "You mean you don't know if it will work?"

"There's only one way to find out!" Nahim stood up and grabbed hold of one of the bricks that made up the word '**Search**'. As soon as he touched it, a tunnel of swirling colours opened up beside them.

"Where does it lead?" Amina asked.

Nahim looked down at Thunderstrike. He was almost upon them. "I've no idea!" he said. "But it can't be any worse than here!" He took a deep breath, jumped into the spinning colours and vanished.

"**I am your master!**" screeched Thunderstrike as he ripped bricks from the line of text below the girls. "**You will serve me!**"

"No way!" Amina shouted. Then she and Polly jumped into the tunnel after Nahim.

Chapter 4
Creepy Crawlies

Travel across the Internet was like nothing the children had ever felt before. They were whisked along the tunnel at top speed, flat on their backs. It was like being on the biggest water-slide in the world.

"Woo-hoo!" Nahim shouted.

"I swear you're enjoying this!" Amina complained.

"Of course I am!" yelled Nahim. "We've escaped from a computer virus and now we're whizzing through cyber-space – this is much better than Mr Lee's boring old ICT class!"

The end of the tunnel rushed towards them and the three of them tumbled out into another room. This one was white, except for a long, thin box that hung in mid-air.

"What is this place?" Amina asked.

"I think it's a search engine," said Polly. "That's what the link said – '**Search**'."

"Cool!" said Nahim. He pulled a marker pen from his pocket and started to write inside the box.

Amina pulled his hand away. "What are you doing?"

"I'm putting my name into the search engine," Nahim told her. "I can find all the places my name comes up on the web. I bet I'm famous!"

"No way!" said Amina. "If this goes wrong – and everything else seems to have gone wrong so far – we could end up with a dozen Nahims running around all over the place. And we don't want that." She spotted Nahim's smile. "I said, we **don't** want that!"

"Oh, all right," moaned Nahim, and rubbed out his name from the search box with his sleeve.

"Maybe we could use the search engine to find a way home," said Polly.

"It's got to be worth a try," Amina agreed. "This may have happened to someone else before us and they could have posted info on the Internet about how to find your way back." She took the marker pen from Nahim and wrote in the search box:

#

How do we get home?

#

"Now what?" Polly asked.

"If you were outside the Net, you'd click on the '**Search**' button," Nahim said, looking around. He hurried over to a rectangle nearby with the word '**GO!**' on it. "Here we go …" He pressed the button as hard as he could.

A hole tore open in the wall next to Amina as if the wall was made of paper and a small, metal spider crawled out.

"Yuck!" Amina cried, as the spider scuttled down the wall. "What's that?"

"A spider," Nahim told her. "That's how search engines find things. They send out little programs called spiders to crawl over the Internet and collect information.

"But they're not supposed to be real spiders though, are they?" said Polly. Another hole ripped open – in the floor this time – and another metal spider clicked out.

"No ..." said Nahim, "but then computer viruses aren't supposed to come to life and attack people!"

Amina heard a noise behind her and spun round. Five – no, six – more holes had torn open and each one had given birth to another silver spider. As they watched, holes began to rip open all around them. "I think we've got a problem!" Amina cried.

"Why?" asked Nahim. "You're not allergic to metal spiders, are you?"

"Don't be stupid!" Amina snapped. Dozens more spiders tore their way into the room. The floor was now a mass of shiny silver bodies as the spiders clambered over one another.

"They're nothing to be scared of," said Nahim. "They collect data from websites, that's all."

"Really?" Amina said. "Then what's that one doing on your arm?"

Nahim yelped and brushed the spider off. It clattered to the floor, landed on its back and whirred madly as its legs tried to flip it the right way up.

Polly felt something on the back of her leg and screamed. Two of the spiders were climbing up her school trousers.

"I told you we had a problem!" said Amina as she knocked half a dozen spiders off her own body. "These things think we're part of the website, and they're trying to find out what we are!"

More and more of the spiders began to crawl up the children's legs. Polly batted at them with her hands, but for every one she knocked off, three more took its place. Within seconds, she, Nahim and Amina were covered from head to toe in the shimmering, clicking creatures.

"Have ... to ... get ... out!" panted Nahim as the spiders began to swarm over his face. The ends of their metal legs dug deep into his skin.

Then the world went black.

Chapter 5
Shop Till You Drop

When Nahim came round, he was lying on a hard, stone floor. He groaned and sat up. "What's going on? Where are the spiders?"

"They've gone," said Amina.

"What? How?"

Amina smiled. "It was Polly," she said. "She stamped on one of them and smashed it open. It turns out they're full of links! We grabbed the first one we saw, it opened up a tunnel and we dragged you in with us."

"Thanks!" Nahim said to Polly, who blushed. "So, where did it bring us out this time?"

"I'm not sure," said Amina. "It looks like some kind of market-place."

Nahim got to his feet and looked around. Amina was right. There were dozens of market stalls, each one piled high with different things. One was covered in pairs of jeans, and another was filled with pots and pans. Others had baby toys, DVDs, coloured pencils and more.

"If this is a market-place," asked Nahim, "where are all the shoppers?"

As if to answer his question, the arm of a huge crane swung down out of the clouds above and sped over the tops of the market stalls until it reached one covered with kettles.

The jaws of the crane clamped around one of the kettles, then lifted it up into the sky and out of sight. Not even a second later, another crane arm swung down and zoomed along a row of tables filled with hundreds of books.

"I think the cranes are the shoppers!" said Amina. She ducked as the arm swept over her head. Other cranes appeared from the clouds and snatched up items of their own.

"This must be one of those auction sites!" said Polly. "My mum uses them all the time to buy stuff for the house. She bids some money on things she wants and, if she has the highest bid when the time is up, she gets them. She got loads of – "

"Look out!" shouted Nahim, and pointed up to a crane arm that had burst through the

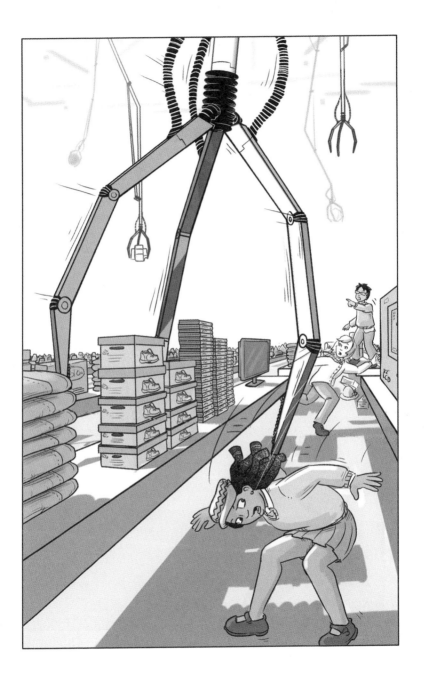

clouds above them. But it was too late. In one swift move, the crane's metal jaws clamped around Polly and lifted her up into the sky.

"Polly!" cried Amina as her friend was carried away. She spun to face Nahim. "Where's it taking her?"

"She is coming to serve ME!" a voice boomed.

"Thunderstrike!" gulped Nahim. "Why is he shopping here?"

"We have to follow Polly!" Amina yelled. "Look – there's another crane heading this way. Jump on it! Now!"

Nahim and Amina jumped into the air as the grabber whooshed past their heads. It grabbed them and they clung on as it lifted them higher and higher. As they passed through the thick clouds, they saw they were swinging towards a huge moving belt like people use in factories. Once they were right above it, the metal jaws of the grabber opened and dropped them onto the belt along with dozens of items shoppers on the auction site had bought.

"Where's Polly?" said Amina. She climbed onto a box of picture frames to get a better view.

"There!" said Nahim. "She's in the middle of a pile of teddy bears."

The pair raced along the belt towards Polly. They had to dodge between racks of fancy dress costumes and jump over packets of babies' nappies, but they reached her just as the items in front of her began to drop off the end of the belt into a huge bag marked **Post**. Polly was hugging one of the teddy bears and crying.

"Time to get out of here," said Nahim as he grabbed Polly's hand and pulled her to her

feet. "You saved me, and now we've saved you!"

"Don't speak too soon!" yelled Amina, as the belt tipped the three of them off the end and into the huge bag below.

Chapter 6
War Zone World

Amina landed on a box full of torches with a CRUNCH. "Is everyone all right?" she called, trying not to think about the poor person who had bought the torches. They weren't going to be happy when the box arrived!

"I'm OK," Polly said. "I landed on a package of net curtains."

The sky disappeared as the postal bag was closed, but then Amina found one of the torches that still worked and switched it on.

"I wish I had landed on curtains!" groaned Nahim. He crawled through the parcels to reach his friends and they saw that his hands and face were smeared in bright blue poster paint. "Why is it always me that gets the messy stuff?" he moaned.

The girls had to laugh. "Well, at least we're on our way home now," said Amina. The packages around them lurched as the bag began to move.

"No," said Nahim. "We have to get out of here! All this stuff is here to be posted. If we stay in the bag, we'll be delivered as well – to Thunderstrike!"

"But what can we do?" asked Polly. "It's not as if we can just wave a magic wand and zap ourselves home."

"Maybe we can!" said Nahim.

Polly looked confused. "What do you mean?"

"Max is a 9th level wizard," Nahim said. "He might be able to cast a spell and get us back to school."

"You mean Max from ICT class?" asked Polly. "He can do magic?"

"Not in real life," said Nahim. "He plays a character in an on-line game called War Zone World. If we can find him there, he might have the power to send us home!"

"Nice idea," said Amina. "But how are we supposed to find a link to War Zone World in here?"

"We don't have to," beamed Nahim. "I'll make one!"

"Make one?" said Polly. "How?"

"Internet links are just groups of letters," said Nahim. "And look at all the parcels around us – they've all got addresses on. If we tear some of the letters off the parcels, I'll be able to use them to write the computer code for a link to War Zone World. Now, I'll need three letter 'w's to begin with …"

For the next 15 minutes, the girls tore letters from the address labels on the parcels around them while Nahim laid them out on a long cardboard box. "There!" he said at last. "That should do it!"

Amina looked at the home-made link:

#

<a href="http://www.warzoneworld.com">
War Zone World</a>

#

"Are you sure that'll work?" she asked. "It just looks like nonsense to me."

"Trust me," said Nahim. "I know how to make website links." He took hold of the girls' hands. "Ready?"

"Let's do it!" smiled Polly. She grabbed hold of the link and the circle of spinning colours opened in front of them again.

"I take back what I said before!" said Amina. "You're not an idiot – you're a genius!"

Nahim smiled. "At long last – my talents have been discovered!" Then the three of them jumped into the tunnel of light together.

This time they were able to stay on their feet as they whizzed along, their arms stretched out to either side to help keep their

balance. "I suppose this is why they call it 'surfing the Internet'!" yelled Polly.

The end of the tunnel raced towards them and they jumped out. They landed in the middle of a forest.

"Is this it?" asked Amina. "Are we in War Zone World?"

"You are indeed!" answered a tiny voice. The children spun round to find a fairy hovering in the air behind them. "You look different to all the other players here," the fairy said. "What kind of strange characters are you?"

"We're elves," said Nahim, with a wink to Polly and Amina. "But we're on a secret quest, and have to stay in disguise."

The fairy buzzed round in a small circle. She seemed to believe him.

"Do you know how we can find a character called Max the Wizard?" asked Amina.

Before the fairy could reply, a dark shadow fell over the forest.

Chapter 7
Max

Thunderstrike crashed through the trees and glared down at the children. "**You should have known you could not escape!**" he bellowed.

"I say!" peeped the fairy. "I've never seen the likes of you around here bef – " With a growl, Thunderstrike snatched the fairy out of the air, stuffed her into his mouth and crunched.

"I think I'm going to be sick!" groaned Amina.

"Well, don't be sick over me!" said Nahim. "I've had enough gunk on me today. Come on – run!"

They all turned and ran deeper into the forest. Thunderstrike chased behind them, ripping up trees by the roots and tossing them over his shoulder like they were little twigs.

"I take back what I took back," Amina shouted at Nahim as she ran. "You're an idiot again!"

"I didn't know that thing would be waiting for us, did I?" cried Nahim. "I thought we could – OW!"

Amina and Polly stopped and turned. Nahim had tripped on a tree root and fallen over. Thunderstrike was rushing towards him, his eyes blazing.

The girls raced back to Nahim. "Get up!" Polly said. "Hurry!"

"I can't!" Nahim said through gritted teeth. "I've twisted my ankle!"

Thunderstrike crashed to a halt in front of the children. "**Now you are mine!**" he roared and reached down with a huge claw.

"Not if I've got anything to do with it!" cried a voice. A lightning bolt shot through the trees and hit Thunderstrike hard in the chest, sending him staggering back.

Amina spun round. "Max!" she cried.

"That's Max?" said Nahim.

The man behind them was tall with long, white hair. He wore deep purple robes and carried a wooden staff. "Hi guys!" he winked.

"Who dares to challenge me?" screeched Thunderstrike, charging towards them again.

Max raised his staff and shot out another bolt of lightning, stronger than the first. It struck Thunderstrike in the stomach. Thunderstrike doubled over and crashed to the ground.

"I am The Great Maximus!" said Max, with a proud smile.

"Yeah!" shouted Nahim. "He's our friend – and he's a 9th level wizard!"

"No, I'm 10th level now," said Max. "While you were gone, I invented a new spell that gave me enough attack points to go up a stage."

"A new spell?" said Polly. "What does it do?"

The Great Maximus strode over to where Thunderstrike was rolling on the ground in agony. He pointed his staff down at the beast. "It mixes magic with anti-virus software!" He fired again. This time the lightning bolt was purple – the same colour as his robes. The charge hit Thunderstrike right between the eyes and the monster screamed ...

... then exploded.

The girls ducked as blood and guts flew up in the air and landed with a splash ... all over Nahim.

"Typical!" Nahim groaned. He picked what looked like a kidney off his face and threw it as far away as he could.

The girls ran over to Max. "Thank you!" cried Amina. "You saved us!"

The Great Maximus spun his staff and smiled. "It was nothing!"

"Can you get us out of here?" asked Polly. "We want to go back to school!"

Nahim climbed to his feet, trying not to put too much weight on his sore ankle. "For once, I agree with the girls," he said.

"You're already there," beamed Max.

Amina looked around. All at once, they weren't in the middle of a forest – they were in their seats in front of their computers in Mr Lee's classroom. It was like they'd never left, only Nahim was covered from head to toe in green saliva, blue poster paint and red monster guts. He slumped into his chair.

"That ... That was amazing!" said Polly.

Max slid the mouse pointer over the 'shut down' button on the screen of his computer and clicked. "Easy when you know how!"

The bell rang to signal the end of the lesson. The children gathered up their bags and headed for the door. That was when Mr Lee spotted the slimy mess all over one of his computer keyboards.

"**Nahim!**" he roared.